THE
ICE BEAR'S
CAVE

To Miranda and Pandora
M.H.

To Alice, Annabel and Harry, with thanks
D.A.

First published in paperback in Great Britain by Collins Picture Books in 2002.

1 3 5 7 9 10 8 6 4 2

ISBN: 0-00-664628-X

Collins Picture Books is an imprint of the Children's Division, part of HarperCollins Publishers Ltd.

Text copyright © Mark Haddon 2002. Illustrations copyright © David Axtell 2002
The author asserts the moral right to be identified as the author of the work.

A CIP catalogue record for this title is available from the British Library.

The HarperCollins website address is: www.fireandwater.com

Printed in Singapore

THE
ICE BEAR'S
CAVE

Mark Haddon

Illustrated by David Axtell

Collins

🔲 *An imprint of HarperCollinsPublishers*

It's six o'clock. Sam licks my face. I wake and rub my eyes.
"What is it, Sam?"
The air is silent, and the room is full of soft blue light.
Suddenly I understand.

We pull the curtains back to find the
village sleeping underneath an eiderdown
of snow.

"Snow," says Robin. "So much snow."
"Alice, look," says Jess, and points.
On the lawn beneath us is a star of paw
tracks where the rabbits came to sit
together in the night.

"Alice," grumbles Mum, "what kind of time is this?"

"It's snowed," I say. "It's like the North Pole!"

Robin bounces on the bed. "No school today!"

"You may be right," says Dad. "The bus will never make it up the hill in this."

Dad takes his shovel from the cupboard in the hall. "I'm going out to clear the drive."

"*We're* going to the North Pole," Jess replies.

"You'll need some breakfast first," says Mum. "The Arctic's pretty cold, this time of year."

The kitchen's like an igloo.
We sit around the table,
eating eggs and toast and
sausages and making
expedition plans.

We put on scarves and hats,

and woolly gloves and wellingtons,

and take the sledge down from the loft.

We find a torch *flashlight* and make some
sandwiches and fill a thermos
flask with cocoa.

"Good luck," says Dad.
"Make sure you don't get lost."
     I tell him Sam will be our husky,
so he'll find the way.

"You never know," says Dad. "You might just come across the Ice Bear's cave."

"The Ice Bear's cave?" asks Jess.

"And then again," he says, "the Ice Bear is a very secret bear who lives beneath the deepest snowdrifts so his cave is rather hard to find."

"Snowdrifts like the snowdrifts on the lawn?" I say.

"Or near the red barn with the rabbit weather vane," shrugs Dad.

"I'm scared of bears," says Robin.

"Don't you worry," Dad says reassuringly. "It's probably a fairy tale…"

We say goodbye. Sam barks. Jess pulls the sledge across the lawn and through the gate. The snow is squeaky-crunchy underneath our feet. The trees are all weighed down with pillows, and our breath is big and steamy in the freezing air.

The morning rushes by.
We climb up Rocket Hill
and slide back down again.

We have a snowball fight. We find the North Pole and we mark it with a flag to prove that we discovered it, and then…

"The rabbit weather vane!" says Jess. "Perhaps we're near the Ice Bear's cave."

The snow begins to fall again.

"I'm cold," says Robin. "Let's go home."

"Let's dig," I say.

I dig, Jess digs, Sam digs, and Robin watches us.

It's almost warm inside our little hole. No wind, no falling snow. The roof above our heads is blue.

We crouch and shovel, slowly scooping out a long white tunnel we can crawl along.

"This is creepy," Robin says.

"Hang on," I say. "We're nearly there."

The snow beneath my hand begins to glow.

There's something on the other side.

"Jess! Come and look at this!" I say.

Jess crawls beside me and we dig together.

The last snow falls away, and suddenly the tunnel opens out
into a high white dome. The Ice Bear sits behind a little table
made of snow. His claws are huge, and round his neck there
is a tartan scarf. His black eyes glitter in the candlelight.
And now I'm frightened. Now I'm really frightened.

Sam barks.

We watch the Ice Bear and he watches us.

At last he speaks.

"And who are you?" His voice is rich and growly, just the way a bear's should be.

"We're Robin, Alice, Jess and Sam," I say. "We didn't mean to wake you up." I want to turn and run, except my legs won't move.

"Well, well…" he says, "you'd better take a seat. I must admit, it's nice to have some company."

I take a seat. Jess takes a seat. But Robin's terrified.

"You, too, little one," the Ice Bear says.

"We've got some sandwiches," says Jess, "and cocoa, too."

Jess pours the mugs of cocoa out, and I hand round the sandwiches.
Food seems to cheer him up. A hot drink and he starts to smile.

"Go on," Jess says, "tell us all about an Ice Bear's life."

"Well, where should I begin…?" he asks.

"Begin with icebergs," Robin says.

"Imagine," says the Ice Bear, "mountains made of frozen water, carved out by the wind and sun, and drifting silently through cold blue seas."

"And are there whales?" asks Robin.

"Whales," he says, "and albatross, walruses and caribou and eider duck… and seals tumbling and turning in the dark beneath the ice floes, chasing fish."

"And is it very dark?" asks Robin.

"Darker than you've ever seen," he says,
"except for when the Northern Lights come out,
and then the whole sky catches fire."

We talk and talk, and finally the Ice Bear notices that Robin is asleep.

"It's getting dark," he says. "Perhaps you should be heading home. And maybe… somewhere in the middle of another winter, when the snow is deep enough to make an Ice Bear's cave, we'll meet again."

The big flakes flash and scatter in the torch beam as we clamber out.

Dad is standing by the red barn with the rabbit weather vane, blowing on his hands.

"Dad… Dad…" says Jess, excitedly, "we saw…"

He puts a finger to his lips. "Why don't you keep it a secret, just between the three of you."

Jess takes Dad's hand and then we wander back towards the lighted house across the squeaky-crunchy snow.

We hang our soggy socks beside
the fire and sip our mugs of soup and
watch the falling flakes come down and down
and talk between ourselves about the Ice Bear.

That night, before I clamber into bed, I take a last look from the window. Everything is still and soft, and somewhere out there, in his cave, the Ice Bear sleeps and dreams of iceberg boats and skies on fire, invisible beneath the cold blue snow.